THE ROOTS THAT GAVE BIRTH
TO MAGICAL BLOSSOMS

A collection of short reflections and accounts
of people's inner thoughts and feelings
2013-2017

Amna Agib (Bit Nafisa)

TSL Publications

First published in Great Britain in 2017
By TSL Publications, Rickmansworth

ISBN / 978-1-911070-70-2

Table of Contents

Foreword

This is my first attempt to write a book in English. Hope it reflects what I would like to convey to you. I want to contribute, in my own way, to healing the suffering of people's souls by telling stories of worries, hopes and expectations in a simple way that relates to everybody. The ideas are based on real live situations but the names don't reflect the origin of the stories.

I dedicate this book to my mother, father, Auntie Fatima (see page 6), the extended family and to Dr Sheik Idris because each of them added special touches that shaped my life in a positive way.

To my son, you have been the source of unlimited motivation without which I might not have been able to do this.

A lot of friends held my hand during this unique journey. They encouraged me, listened to my first drafts and gave me useful and honest feedback.

A special thank you to Pat and Julie, Ben and Jack, my son's friends — you splashed a lot of fun which I do appreciate.

Thank you to Harrow Writers' Circle who unlocked my potential, gave me the encouragement and boosted my confidence to be where I am so far. My special appreciation goes to John Monaghan for his invaluable advice and Indra for his persistence in pushing useful information into our 'mail boxes'.

I also thank those who crossed my path and gave up their valuable time to explore a bit of my soul ... my writings. Thank you, Sharon, James, Dawn, Phyllis and others for the encouragement I needed.

And to those who intentionally or unconsciously hurt me, I say, you helped me come back stronger than ever.

Thank you.

To your soul Auntie Fatima

On Saturday 12 August 2017, you peacefully passed away leaving a great legacy for the women of the world and vulnerable people of the earth. People from across the world paid tribute to you not to mention your family, colleagues, Governments and the lay people.

The Guardian wrote: 'The Sudanese feminist and political activist Fatima Ahmed Ibrahim, who has died aged 88, was a force of nature. To observe her in action was to be humbled by her indefatigability. In a country where the slightest of strays from social convention were frowned upon, she was a pioneer in the field of women's rights, and, in 1965, became Sudan's first female member of parliament after participating in a democratic movement that removed military rule.'

The Times described you as an 'outspoken' woman who was 'never shy about speaking her mind'. They told of your achievement years ago when your school cancelled science classes as inappropriate for girls and how you promptly organised the strike that led to them being reinstated.

In addition, your death reminded the world about your husband, the trade union leader Al-Shafi Ahmed al-Sheikh, who was tortured and executed in 1971.

Rest in peace Auntie Fatima and remember your children and grandchildren will carry on your legacy like the magical blossoms that keep the roots alive.

The Roots that gave Birth
to Magical Blossoms

This story is about influential men and women, their children and grandchildren, who lived in a small village in the heart of Africa.

The importance of their role to society mirrored that of the roots to the survival of a tree. They provided the support and stability not only for their children but for the community as a whole. Just like the roots as they dig deep into the earth to secure their place within the plant kingdom, those men and women won their place in the heart of the social structure.

Many generations at that time lived under restricted rules and practices. There was no comprehensive education. The majority of men were illiterate, not to mention the women who were housebound and totally dependent on their husbands and fathers.

However, this particular family was one of the luckiest families. All had their share of intelligence and deep knowledge especially in the area of religion. They inherited wisdom and commitment and earned respect and a credible position among their community. They were original and distinctive among their fellows. They lived a pure and natural life protecting the young, supporting the weak and respecting the elders. Honest and joyful, harsh but rewarding was their path. Peaceful and fulfilling was their destiny.

This family faced a lot of challenges that helped them to be more relevant to people's hopes as they conquered the world but evolved at home.

Aiming at perfection they suffered a lot. However, they overcame their fears and satisfied people's expectations. Success was their limit and achievement was their hope.

During their struggle for a better life for their community they stood tall and proud and won the battle. Those men and women formed the foundation for a liberal movement in their country.

Their children and grandchildren inherited an open-minded approach and liberalism. Many of them became beacons in local, national and international arenas. The headmaster, the religious leader, the politician, the ordinary ones and the mothers, all were leaders in their own rights. Their intelligence was a gift from God.

The wives, mothers and daughters were exceptionally talented, intelligent, delightful, sober but strong characters. They were a collection of miracles. Together they faced the impossible and achieved their goals. They were an inspiration to follow. Their names were printed as precious badges of honour on the face of their nation's history and beyond.

When winter comes and the trees cry their leaves off, the roots glow in a magical way. They guide the wanderer around. Their effect echoes the power of a tiny light at the heart of the sea when it defeats the anger of the storm and leads the helpless to the safety of the shores.

But then the storm dies out and the shining light is apparently forgotten as the sounds of life dominate the scene, yet the sparkle of the roots remains. It never dies or shies away. It continues to tell the story of each individual, such as the story of Ahmed who became the first native headmaster for the only primary school for boys. He was appointed by the governor general. In the school, he was not addressed by his name. He was called 'the headmaster' as a sign of respect as in village culture the young are not allowed to address the older generation by their name. So 'the headmaster' later became his nickname within the community including his family.

He was a spiritual leader, who led the prayers five times a day. The entire adult male population in the village, except the very sick, attended the daily prayers, standing shoulder to shoulder behind him in massive rows.

This position was deemed the most prestigious. It required that the position-holder gain the trust of almost every member of the community regardless of their age and gender; the traders, the politicians, the professionals, the governors, the lay people and mothers and their children.

At the heart of the darkness when the country was under foreign occupation and the slave trade was booming, the headmaster lived with a glimpse of light, the knowledge and wisdom, which were the only treasure he cherished for his family to inherit.

At that time, women had no rights. They were required to obey their husbands, fathers and brothers without argument. Women were perceived as a liability, 'inconvenient truth' and means for a secret pleasure.

Ahmed had three intelligent daughters: Medina, Batool and Asia. They were roughly between six and nine years old with a year gap between each of them.

The three girls were well disciplined. They were always well dressed in neat white national costumes, which covered the whole of their tiny bodies and their hair. They never left their house unaccompanied.

There were no schools for girls and they were not allowed to join the religious schools, which only taught religion and language to help the pupils to read the holy book and perform their religious duties.

On one hand, the only source to gain a wider knowledge and learn new skills, which are essential for daily life, was a tiny shy classroom for boys. It was lacking basic furniture and equipment. Pupils sat on hand-made wool rugs which their mothers made. On the other hand, girls were taught by their mothers inside their homes how to cook, clean, sew and bring up children.

The headmaster hesitated to go against the strong and influential social norms to educate his daughters outside the approved essences. He had long and deep conversations with his cousin Yuseif, who had always been his loyal friend, and the hand that supported him in difficult times.

'My friend, someone has to lead the change,' Yuseif stressed to Ahmed, 'and that is you.'

'Do you think men will easily give up their upper hand position?' Ahmed directed his question towards his cousin but continued, 'Even the women themselves will fight against us.'

'I do not want to put my family under strain.'

Yuseif laughed, 'I did not know that you were so soft inside.'
Ahmed quickly replied in a defensive way, 'What do you think? I am a human being first and my family is my responsibility. I need to protect them.'

He quickly returned to the subject of girls' education. 'Do you really know what the impact of our plan is? We could end up in exile.'

'Could you bear that?'

'We would be shunned and reviled for the rest of our lives and the lives of our future generations.'

After long considerable deliberations with himself he decided to follow his instinct and share his treasure, education, with his three precious girls, knowing that Yuseif would always support him.

Yuseif had a great talent in attracting and influencing people, even in the most critical situations. He had a sense of humour that diffused the most intense moments.

Ahmed raised his bare hands against the destructive waves of anger and the deadly flames of disgrace that leaped from all the eyes around him when he admitted his daughters to the boys' school and allowed them to sit in the same class with the boys.

During the short time the girls stayed in the school they always felt isolated, but stayed resilient.

For the father it was the fiercest struggle of his entire life, with almost all sectors of the community, including women, who rejected his ill-perceived action.

The parents threatened to pull their children out of the school. His fellow teachers totally ignored the presence of the girls in their lessons. Men deserted and stopped attending his prayers; the most hurtful thing to happen to a religious leader. Neighbours banned their wives and daughters from visiting his home. His life and that of his family had suddenly become a target for everybody.

It was the worst psychological war he and his family had to go through. They felt vulnerable and exposed. But with the moral support of his wife, Hawa, and Yuseif, he never minded what had happened. He only saw the opportunity for his daughters to shine against the odds and for his dream, to educate them, to come true, paving the way for a prosperous future for generations to come.

The family became stronger and closer to each other. The young girls were well supported. Ahmed continued to pray with Yuseif only until few relatives and friends joined in following Yuseif's hard work and persuasion.

On the first day of school in a strange and hostile environment, Medina, Batool and Asia were all frightened to death. They felt as if they had shrunk to sub-zero level but were over the moon about standing shoulder to shoulder with the boys. Asia, the youngest cried her eyes out and every boy in the class teased and laughed at her.

The girls were literally stuck with each other and avoided any contact with the boys. They did not talk to or even glance at any of their classmates. They sat at the back of the classroom on wooden chairs which were made especially for them.

During the breaks they went home and came back after the boys had settled in. They were always accompanied by the maid, Sara, who waited for them at the door of the classroom. She was their bodyguard and chaperon.

The boys looked at the three charming girls, in their attractive white dresses, as a source of holy radiance, though they saw them as a thread of a threat. They looked up to them but down on them at the same time.

Boys claimed that the superiority of man on earth was a given fact and assumed that the house was the natural place for girls. Hence, they did not welcome the stars' presence. Some of them were unable to accept the fact that girls were among them and stopped coming to school, whilst others respected them for their good manners.

A minority of the pupils went an extra mile to annoy the three sisters in attempts to drive them out of the school. They threw ink on their white costumes, put sugar on their chairs to attract ants and sometimes tried to intimidate and physically restrain them. The behaviour of some pupils was appalling.

The ones who thought the worst about the girls dared not express their feelings in the open, because the girls were perceived as the headmaster's property.

Sara protected them as well as she could but chose not to tell the headmaster everything for fear that he might pull them out of the school. She could tell by the look in their eyes and their gentle smiles that they enjoyed being in the school despite all the trouble caused by the jealous boys.

The word spread around faster than the speed of light, 'the man in charge betrayed the village.'

However, he stood solidly by his choice. With his hand on his heart he believed that he was guided by the prophet's spirit, who once instructed his followers to take half of their religious knowledge from his wife, the mother of all believers.

'This should be right,' Ahmed convinced himself. 'I had a clear indication from God.' This vision was the only comfort he had during the hardest journey of his life pursuing his dream to educate his daughters.

He felt strangely calm and extremely determined to complete his heartfelt mission. He tried to persuade others to follow his footsteps but they ignored his call and turned their backs on him. Nobody wanted to listen or speak to him. They abandoned him although he had been their popular and respected leader. He was the one who held their hands through all their difficult and dark days together, during a significantly harsh and unpleasant era when their country was ruled by foreigners.

The country's governors heard the rumour flying around: 'the headmaster has gone mad. He encourages sin in the daylight, by allowing his daughters to mix with boys.'

Deep down the foreigners felt happy for the crack on the horizon, which would weaken the resistance against their regime, but they needed to be seen considering people's views and listening to their concerns. They were desperate to win both sides. They had to compromise to win hearts and minds.

They reluctantly agreed to move the three girls to their educational establishment, although it was normally forbidden for the natives to even pass by the foreigners' territory. Their compounds were surrounded by heavily armed guards.

For the nation, that step was the real birth of three shooting stars who cemented the way for a brighter future for the women's movement, though they died because of the intensity of the darkness around them. The pressure was so powerful that their souls were unable to bear it.

Medina, the eldest, died suddenly as her heart stopped beating with no regrets for what she and her sisters had achieved for women all over the world. They became role models and a national treasure. Their footsteps had been followed by women in every corner of the globe.

Batool, died giving birth to a son due to a shortage of medical supplies.

And Asia, contracted a rare form of cancer, which claimed her young life. The people in the village believed that the corrupt government compromised people's health and received a huge benefit for that. At the same time many innocent lives were lost for unexplained reasons. This phenomenon had suddenly increased among people, including children.

The story of the girls' life and death is to be told as long as life exists. It enriched the history of humankind in a unique way. It remains a milestone for each mother-daughter bond, not only in that remote part of the world.

They were acknowledged as heroines, because they were able to touch the unreachable and thus laid out the first block of a long-standing solidarity within the most disadvantaged sector of the human community, the women of the world.

The achievements of the roots and their descendants are historical icons that tell the story of the struggle for dignified life and will do so for generations to come.

My Promise to Nafisa

Nafisa was the one who changed my life for ever. She was strong, open-minded, kind and always put people first. She was well edu-cated whilst the majority of women were confined to their own homes. She went through the death passage time and time again whenever she gave birth. Her pregnancies were complicated by her underlying condition. She survived the ordeal until one sad day she died alone in her hospital bed, after the hospital visiting time.

Nafisa grew up in a unique family, where every individual was a record breaker in one way or another. She chose her way of life, which was not necessarily blessed by those around her. She walked through her tough life with her head held high. She had a warm heart and welcoming nature. Nafisa sacrificed a lot knowing that her work would pay off somehow.

Nafisa remained the source for holding her entire family together during both her life and after her death. She was the hope that guided her family during the darkest moments of their lives and was a devoted daughter, wife, sister, mother and friend.

She was kind enough to always give her last portion of food to total strangers who knocked at her door desperate for a piece of bread in tough times.

Her family were proud of the courage that she had inherited from her parents and grandparents.

She gained great insight into people's needs and won for them a long battle that changed their lives for the better. She shone in a complicated political and social environment. She acted in both the front line and behind the scenes.

Nafisa helped influential men and women to preserve the dignity of their families, communities and the country. No wonder there is a saying, 'educate a mother and you will educate a nation.' And Nafisa was a nation.

I left my country at a young age chasing her dream for me. I landed in a place, which was so remote from home, with no luggage but my hopes. People described that place as 'a country with offbeat birds', referring to the lack of communication with the rest of the world.

At first, a lot of things seemed so bizarre even the order of their names. Our official national records identify a person by his first name, followed by the father's name and the grandfather's, and so on.

At the airport an immigration officer asked me about my family name. But I didn't have one. They created one for me. Since then my grandfather's name has become my family name. Most of the time I didn't respond when people called my surname as it is a male name and I hadn't got used to the fact that it was my new name. That was the first time I started to realise that I had lost my identity and sense of belonging.

I was puzzled by many other things and people were puzzled by the colour of my skin. They were curious to know whether the colour of my blood is red and the colour of cow's milk in my country is white. They do not even know where my country is.

I was particularly astonished about this as we learned in school about other countries; their history, geography, industry and foreign policies. Maybe that is not the case in countries in other parts of the world.

The citizens, though, were very friendly and nowhere near being racist. It was just they hadn't seen dark-skinned people before. As they got to know us they treated us as one of their own.

My friends and I were shocked to learn that the shower facilities were communal where all the females in the building shared the showers which had no privacy. We decided to have our slot at midnight when every other person was fast asleep.

I was surrounded by mountains of snow on my way to anywhere outside the hostel. I put on my entire wardrobe but was still shivering and felt frozen just like a chicken in my freezer. Actually we didn't have freezers. We suspended the shopping bags outside the windows and the meat became as solid as steel.

In our Institute there were students from all over the world. We felt a strong bond between us; suffered, struggled and achieved together. We dressed in each other's national costumes and spoke a common foreign language. We sang international songs, performed diverse folklore dances, and even laughed at jokes from all over the globe.

All of us at one point missed our homes and families and cried when it was dark, misty and cold. Sometimes we felt empty. However, it was an amazing journey and we had unbelievable luck.

My life is blessed apart from the fact that I hardly feel like I belong anywhere. I even enjoy the feeling of being a stranger wherever I settle. I suffered from a kind of identity crisis, though I learned a lot of skills and gained valuable experience. I designed my own coping mechanisms. I had the opportunity to visit different countries and live amongst various communities. That was a treasure to be drawn upon whenever I felt low.

These memories accompanied me throughout my life before I finally settled in another island far from home.

My dreams were shattered at times. My beliefs were overwhelmed by a lot of issues around me and my joy was ripped apart but the spirit of Nafisa was still alive in me. I stood against unfairness and all the odds. I literally shared my soul with others who have no voice or choice. I developed a sustained resilience when faced with horrible, inhumane, man-made situations. Deep down I feel I have won.

When I look back at my journey, I appreciate the fact that Nafisa always had confidence in me and I didn't want to let her down. I was lucky to be part of her life.

I made a promise to her that I will be there for the needy. I will be 'her' for my children and the children of the world.

By documenting her story I feel that I have rewarded her memory and kept my promise. I feel that her existence has given me an unlimited ability to love and forgive.

I count myself as one of those luckiest children of the earth, who have been part of Nafisa's rich life at one point. There were many people who were connected to her in a unique way, including the biological bond.

Nafisa's fingerprints are stamped on each step I take in life; my childhood, educational achievements, employment, and my social and personal successes, to date.

God bless her in her eternal life.

Walking the Corridor

of Power

Mustafa was born with an orange colour of skin. Since he was a baby he felt that he was different; dreamed differently and suffered in silence. He had a unique mentality and coping mechanism which no one could understand. He was very quiet, hesitant and indecisive. He absorbed pain to the extent that he had frequent episodes of unexplained blackouts.

The doctors diagnosed his condition as unexplained habitual reactions. His episodes remained that way, as his secret was kept deeply buried in his sub-conscious. Only he recognised that this was how he coped when things turned hideous, time and time again. So, he lived as a stranger within his own soul. His mental capacity was labelled as below normal by the 'socially' accepted measures. Strangely enough, he always felt that the 'socially' accepted measures were far below his standard.

His family loved him in a strange way. Provided the best for him but something was always missing and he couldn't put his finger on it. He went on with his life as normally as he could, in the circumstances, but always his soul wondered in his own world of imagination. In a way he lived his dreams on a totally different level till he stepped into the 'corridor of power', the killer of souls and dreams.

Where are you Ms Jane and Mr Kief in the crowd? Please wave at me to see you. This message is for you, though it may be relevant to many. I was asked to deliver their version of speech to tell you my personal happy story. What a story and what an approach.

I just want to say sorry for not getting in touch since I took my first step in the corridor. They will not allow us. They are monitoring me now. You will be pleased to hear that I am still breathing, though I lost a big chunk of my soul. It was thrown in the bureaucratic recycling bin, as it doesn't fit with the ever low assumptions.

Please be assured I am still there against all odds, clutching the slippery throat of the corridor and crawling under the skin of the self-appointed guards. It is a very strange place to be in. I thought, or in fact believed, I am dreaming but I always smell the sound of your drums. Yes I smell the sound filling the place, right now ... your cry, whispers and your fears. I hear your oppressed smiles. Don't be surprised. Here, in the corridor, there is no sense of the senses. I always hug your laughter when I feel lonely and cold and touch your frustrations with my bare hands to keep me warm. They train us to do strange things. I am not sure what is expected of us. Hope not what I imagine.

You know the guards tried once to bleach my skin but I forcefully resisted. My body defence mechanisms were strangely over-powered. Ms E, Mrs S and Mr A, I saw your bodies lying side by side between my skin and the bleach. Thank you. Don't ask me how. No wonder that is the corridor of power!

You know when you enter; there is no prospect of getting out. It is a trap. Hope I never listened to their propaganda that we will have everything the moment we join them. We joined based on their powerful but false promises. I regret that now, but I wanted to taste how to be rich and in power. I wanted to overcome my problems. I thought I would be in a better situation. I promised my family to have whatever they dreamed of for very many years, as I took the decision.

I am so confused I need to ask you this ... do you see through me? Do you see me in a peculiar way? I mean ... how do I put this? ... do you see me? ... aah ... I mean naked? Why I am asking? Because, here, we see the same things you see in a different shade of colour. By the way, what are we celebrating today? Why I am talking to you? Do we celebrate our destiny, resilience, our standing still, our shared history, our being oddly recruited or our mutilated power of conscious and minds ...? I don't know, the guards have deliberately concealed that from us all. It seems it is a top secret ... It is their term; don't ask, don't feel, don't see, don't hear, just do what you are asked to do.

Oh ... soooory I have to go now as I was reminded that I forgot who I am and that I exceeded the capacity I should operate within, which is enough to demonstrate their flexibility and authenticity to the outside world.

Maybe I get in touch if I survive the last leg of crossing the corridor to the unknown.

Be well ... be safe ... you know ... don't listen to them. Remember I just told you my personal story through their dense lenses to make them happy and avoid the unbelievably harsh punishment.

Thank you for listening.

Fight or Flight

'Boys do not cry'. That was the way Mohamed and his generation were taught. They were led to believe that tears are the girls' weapon and that boys had bows and arrows. They wondered why?

There was a clear cut line between blue and pink but for Mohamed there wasn't. This fact influenced all the stages of his life.

Mohamed was admitted to a secure psychiatric hospital after he tried to take his own life.

His doctor, Adam, took him to a quiet room and encouraged him to tell the story of his life.

Mohamed spent a long time just staring at the ceiling. Suddenly, he started to throw unconnected words and phrases together as he looked straight into his doctor's eye and started telling his story.

It was clear to Adam that Mohamed was in great psychological pain and he needed to release that pain somehow.

'You know, we were told that tears are women's mechanism to cope. Men have to survive without this mechanism. We have to fight whilst women choose the flight route. What a wonder the world is!' Mohamed started his conversation.

'I realised that women suffer on a daily basis and they cope. They are the strongest ones. They absorb all kinds of pain, but live longer.'

'My wife was an exception. She left us so young. One bright day I glanced at her curled up in her bed. She looked very peaceful, pretty and glowing like *Sleeping Beauty*.

'I didn't realise that she was melting like a piece of butter in the heart of a heated pan. I was left devastated by her death. Since then I have struggled on my own. I was unable to share my grief or to let it go. I have preserved it untouched for my whole life.'

Mohamed cried for a while before he continued. 'I always wondered why men have tears if they can't wash their eyes from inside-out.

'Men have the power, the brain and the sense of direction. They are led to believe that they are the leaders and women are the followers. Men decide the fate of the world. Aren't they the warriors, the hunters, the tribal chiefs and the businessmen? They are also the military personnel and the presidents.'

Without disruption Mohamed carried on, 'Women look after men's needs, homes, sons and honour. They don't come cheap. Men buy them with flowers, gold, cars and Euros and pour out their hearts and pockets when they get married.'

Mohamed took a deep breath. 'A teacher once mentioned that the origin of the word woman is a womb of a man.'

I was astonished.

'Did you know that?' Mohamed turned his head to where the doctor was sitting. Adam remained silent.

'Anyway,' Mohamed continued, 'this reflects the historical hidden and unspoken testimonies that women were created as child-carriers only.

'Believe me that was the case even in many developed countries.

'When women joined the labour market, they were pushed back very hard. Employers used women's biological characteristics such as pregnancy as a reason to exclude them in favour of their male work-fellows. Male co-workers are better paid and more readily promoted.

'I couldn't understand the saying behind every successful man is a woman.' Mohamed laughed loudly. He drank a glass of water and wiped his lips repeatedly. He appeared agitated.

The doctor encouraged him to carry on. Mohamed felt a bit more comfortable and moved his chair forward.

'Do you really believe that men need women's guidance to flourish?' Without waiting for an answer, he continued, 'Are women the real leaders on earth? My personal experience confirms that but the social norms do not approve it.

'For all these years I was left totally confused about which message we need to grasp and accept as our value. I repeatedly lost control, although I was expected to act as the wise man, the role model for my male offspring.

'Have you come across something like that?'

Adam smiled at him to convince him that he was not alone. This gesture persuaded him to carry on revealing his story. 'When life gets harder and responsibilities bite, things turn ugly and we direct our disappointments, failures and frustrations towards our loved ones.'

Adam noted that Mohamed was very cautious revealing this information, which implied that he had a sense of guilt.

'Many act in a nasty manner, though sometimes they might not be aware of the impact of their acts. They are just releasing the accumulated energy in their muscles. When the moment settles they cry their souls out and are forgiven.'

Mohamed took a deep breath, stood up and walked towards the door as if he was running away from a long forgotten memory or a horrible dream.

'Apparently life continues as usual till it reaches a breaking point, when there is no turning back.' He concluded.

Mohamed sat down again. He looked at his doctor and threw at him a series of questions without expecting any interaction from the doctor.

'Should men feel ashamed or is this the norm?'

'Do you call this living a double life?'

'Is this situation well known to the clinician or is it just a social phenomenon?'

Mohamed was convinced that whatever the situation the impact of these acts was immense. He just needed to spit it out.

Mohamed told his doctor that he had made a commitment to himself and had made a great effort to understand other people's behaviour and his own as well. He explained that although he inherited a lot of unique qualities from his father and grandfather, he learnt a lot from his mistakes. He acknowledged that he was influenced by many other factors during his controversial journey.

He shook his head and whispered, 'I was a great person in the eyes of strangers, close family and friends but I barely recognised that fact myself.'

To ease the situation, Adam tapped Mohamed on the shoulder. 'Are you tired? We can continue another time.'

Ignoring the question Mohamed carried on, 'I grew up with a hidden kindness. I cried when I was away from the crowd and felt relieved.

'I stored a huge amount of emotion inside my body. The energy had built up in my muscles beyond normal capacity. It didn't stop urging my brain to be released. It created a dilemma between acting or not.'

Mohamed raised the tone of his voice whilst his breathing became shallow and more frequent.

'I am the brave ... I am the leader and the family backbone. I am ...'

He then whispered gently, 'Listen to me. Who am I? I am a lie wrapped in a truth.'

His eyes were filled with tears. He continued without wiping them away and took a deep breath after each sentence.

'Life passed by.

'The reasoning had left.

'I no longer had the power.'

With a trembling high-pitched voice he reversed this statement, 'No, I am still the achiever though.

'I passed my strong genes down the line. They are the strongest, the dominant and the ones in control.'

Mohamed suddenly felt exposed and vulnerable. Looking at his feet, he said, 'You know the situation has changed.' He pointed at his grey hair and smiled, 'Look at my hair, it has faded away. My teeth are no longer my own.'

With more enthusiasm he stated, 'The energy, though, is still growing inside my muscles and is desperate to be released.

'Should I? I always hesitated, but I can hear the shout even now, "just do it".

'I am in a real mess.'

Mohamed described himself as being kind of in the shadow. He added that he wanted to declare the sense of duty that haunted him all his life. He felt he was responsible for safeguarding man's kindness and the source of tears.

Mohamed looked directly at his doctor and asked, 'Can I?' Five minutes of silence passed. Mohamed asked again, 'Am I allowed?' He begged for an answer.

'Yes of course,' the doctor replied.

Mohamed started talking to himself. 'Do I fight? ... I am frail ... Do I choose the flight route? My pride will not allow me to do so.'

Mohamed held his head with both hands and shouted loudly, 'Fight ... Flight.'

Bang! he hit the table.

'I am exhausted.'

His voice started to diminish and was hardly heard beyond his throat, 'I lost my gentle soul. I lost ... I can't remember.

'My pure natural feelings? Maybe.

'My ability to understand, or even myself?

'I do not know.

'My dignity has gone.'

He looked at the ceiling and continued, 'I once cried as I had never done before. That moment resembled my first cry when my head passed through the "passage to life" leaving my mum's womb forever.'

Mohamed looked straight ahead and seemed confused.

'Why has the noise suddenly stopped? It is terribly quiet. I am numb and heavy.

'Is this how your soul leaves your body?

'I am breathing though.

'Am I on the path out of life?

'Everything goes in circles: the sun, the moon, the seasons, the day and night. Even the flat earth was proven to be round.

'Is this my circle or just a nightmare?

'Is this what is meant to happen or made to happen?'

At that moment Mohamed recalled his belief that his uniqueness was about feeling free outside people's normal comfort zones. He once described it as when he allows himself to swim away from the force of gravity and the factual accounts of real life. It is when he feels that limitless and intense thing, which he can't put his finger on, expand beyond his imagination. He wondered whether he was hallucinating or he was really in that state.

A gentle sob filled the air. 'It was so hard on me. My life was built around my beloved one. I cannot imagine my life beyond the cemetery.

'Everything was beautiful and well arranged.

'Dust ... to dust ... Amen.'

'I am not sure whether my journey has come to an end or it has just started. I have been strangled by loneliness and emptiness.

'God help me. Amen.'

After that intense session with Adam, Mohamed appeared so calm and confident. He smiled at his doctor and left the room.

A Scene at the Surface

of My Memory

Malika lived with her family in a village somewhere in the bleeding heart of the world. This could have been in Somalia, Rwanda, Sudan, Libya, Iraq, Syria or even Ukraine. It doesn't matter where and when and how. She was a bright happy little school girl until her country was torn apart by a long-standing war that destroyed the cities and villages alike.

The school in her village was damaged beyond repair, driving kids onto the streets. Homes were set on fire scattering families to the outskirts of the village. Men had to fight without prior knowledge of using firearms and most of them were killed. Boys were kidnapped and exploited as child soldiers. Mothers were used as human shields and the motherless babies were left crawling across the fire lines sucking their thumbs. Innocent young girls were raped and forced into prostitution.

With time the food supplies dried out. No hospitals were left standing to care for the wounded and the sick. They lost all their medical supplies and buildings. The streets were saturated with the smell of death. The ghosts were wandering in the deserted homes in daylight. The darkness dressed their beautiful village and stole its spirit. It was no longer full of life, celebrations or pride. No people there to care about each other.

The village failed to absorb all that and wondered if the cause of the chaos was a search for power, clash of values and beliefs or human greed and hatred. Nobody had an answer. And the impact was beyond the imagination. The village had gone for ever.

The village was once known for respecting its entire people and its citizens worked together like those in an ant kingdom. They lived within their means: cultivating their own food, making their dairy products and keeping hens and cattle. They had their natural remedies and built their own social and economic fabric. Life went so well until the war spread out like fire engulfing each corner and edge of their country; but the world around them was numb, unable to see, hear or feel. The screams of the dying had lost their way whilst many were so busy counting the profit and expanding the limit of their power.

Malika had miraculously managed to cross the border, the only survivor among a large group of men and women who fled the conflict. Her baggage was a collection of sweet memories. She grabbed her mum and dad's hands and hopped like a bunny, giggled as a squirrel gathering the wild yellow, red and purple flowers. She carefully clipped them with coloured pins on her head scarf. She sang her beloved melody, closed her eyes and whispered 'good night mammy'. Instead of the soft and kind voice of her mum's 'good night sweetheart,' a sudden high-pitched blast filled the whole space. She held her head between her knees and forcefully pressed her ears to block the distressing noise and covered her eyes to keep them shut to avoid the flash of light that filled the horizon. Her tears flowed all over her face.

Then a deadly silence unmercifully squashed her tiny body to the point that she thought she would shatter into pieces. In a moment she was surrounded by static, lifeless and cold bodies piled on top of each other. Though she was paralysed by the scene, she started to run as if she was chased by a tiger. Her heart was racing her breathing. Her body was covered with sweat. Her tongue hung out of her mouth. Her legs towed behind her body. Her clothes smelled of fresh blood reminding her of the smell she most hated when she accompanied her mother to the butcher's shop on their daily trip during her school holiday.

For the first time, she believed what her teacher told her in the lessons, that the earth is round and not flat as her young mind perceived. Her head was spinning exactly as her headmaster described how the earth rotates around the sun, with no prospect of reaching a finish line. The sky was grey and thick over her head. She prayed and prayed for God until she lost consciousness.

When she was able to open her eyes, a week after, she was convinced that she had a nightmare. The faces surrounding her were unfamiliar. 'She might have eaten a lot and gone straight to bed against her mum's advice'. She drifted into a deep sleep. When she was alert she saw smiley friendly faces which she didn't recognise. She touched her face to ensure that she was alive. A woman greeted her, 'Welcome back. You are safe here. You are lucky. You were brought to us by a kind man who found you nearby.' But she understood nothing as she was confused, extremely tired and vulnerable.

Malika could barely breathe or speak. She was severely dehydrated and covered with blood and cuts. Her clothes were hanging by the shoulder only. Her body temperature was dangerously high.

Huda, the camp's volunteer manager was a nurse. She took care of Malika until her condition had improved.

A long time passed before she realised what had happened to her and how she ended up in the refugee camp which was set up to prevent those who had escaped from the war entering the neighbouring cities. Malika learned that her father, mother, brothers and sisters were missing. She asked Huda whether there was another camp, hoping that the rest of her family might have been saved. It was the hardest thing Huda had to explain to a terrified little girl that the rest of her family were not accounted for. Malika was unable to talk or walk following this revelation. She stopped eating as well. She was fed through a tube that hung from her nose, which she pulled out most of the time during the agitated state she was in. She gave Huda a hard time re-installing it, as if she was lost the will to live.

The conditions in the camp were far less than acceptable. But they had no other or better choice. In the circumstances they saw the camp as luxurious; sleeping on paper rags, taking shelter from the sun using cardboard boxes and hearing no sound of explosions. They divided the responsibilities between themselves and helped each other. Strangely, they felt well settled together. They were a mixture of men and women, old and young, strong and weak, kind and mean but a special bond was felt among them.

Life went by with no sense of day or night, month or year for Malika and most of the residents until that night.

Malika was laying down staring at nothing when she heard a movement. She was frozen by the unexpected surprise; a new room-mate entered her sleeping area. It was a shadow of her mum. Both, nearly skeletons, fell into each other's shaky arms and embraced one another for what seemed nine months' length, the time they had spent apart. Malika giggled as a squirrel and started singing her beloved melody, closed her eyes and whispered, 'Love you mammy'. To her surprise and disbelief, the kind and soft voice oozed like a shy stream through her ear: 'I love you too baby'. She was the youngest daughter. She sniffed her mother's body and felt her lungs were expanding beyond the entire camp reaching their village at its original state.

Suddenly, they heard a loud uproar. They thought the war had caught up with them in this holy moment. Their bodies had just melted, remodelled and fused into an eternal soul. Soon enough they realised that it was just a helicopter throwing cans of food, loaves of bread and basic medical supplies to the camp's forgotten population. People stumbled over each other's heads catching the falling parcels. The food was so different to that they used to eat, but did it matter? Mother fed Malika in her mouth just like a pigeon feeding her new-born chicks. No wonder Malika was re-born in that moment.

After a couple of heavenly months for Malika and her mum, three helicopters arrived at the refugee camp. Well-dressed people stepped out. Their chief addressed the camp's residents, 'We are pleased to inform you that we are able to transfer some of you to a better place. However, we are unable to accommodate all of you.' He could see the disappointment in the eyes around him. It was a tough decision.

With the help of Huda they classified and sorted the group according to their age and state of health. They picked Malika amongst others. Her mother stepped out to join her daughter.

'I am sorry ma'am, we are going to take the young girls, the elderly and the sick only.'

'But she is the only child left. I lost her once but can't let her go now. We had just re-united after I lost hope. Take both of us or none,' a weak voice objected but was lost in the crowd.

'Please use your discretion. You can't tear a family apart like the cruel and reckless war. Both were so traumatised.' Huda begged the officer in charge.

'Sorry, we follow clear instructions. We have targets to meet and other things to do,' he replied with no sign of emotion, humanity or empathy.

Malika ignored the instructions. She didn't want to go without her mother. The chief ordered the other men to drag the girl to the helicopter. Malika resisted as much as her tiny body permitted. She was pushed forcibly inside.

Soon the three helicopters left leaving those who remained confused. Malika looked through the small window with tears flowing all over her face. She wanted to stay with her mother or at least hug her goodbye. She saw her mother chasing the rising helicopter through the dense cloud of dust which was generated by its departure.

'I am just a number, a target but no one.' Malika shut her eyes and slipped into a deep sleep to wipe out her agony.

Malika and the others were led into a huge building, where men and women dressed in similar white or blue outfits were moving fast in and out the rooms. She was asked to open her mouth, take off her clothes and take a deep breath. She cried loudly and refused to take her clothes off in front of a strange man. 'My dad would kill him if he knew what he had asked me to do,' she thought. 'He must be out of his mind,' she murmured and curled into the bed holding on tight to her clothes. The man in the uniform was unable to understand why she refused to take off her clothes. He was frustrated. However, a lady who spoke Malika's language gently held her hand. 'He is a doctor and would like to make you feel better,' she explained.

'Do not worry I will be with you all the time.' Malika felt assured and then reluctantly allowed the doctor to examine her. He smiled at her and she smiled back.

With time Malika felt healthier and happier apart from that ugly fragment which was trapped inside her forever; the scene of her mother running after the rising helicopter. It kept pushing itself to the surface of her memories and remained there for the rest of her life.

Malika learnt that there was a big organisation that arranged their transfer from the camp to this city and supported their accommodation in a hostel nearby. She lived in a room with three other girls, who she didn't know before. All felt connected in a way; they spoke the same language and went through the same experience of the war and the camp. They felt like one family. They had bad and good times together. She proudly called them sisters.

When she just felt connected again, she was told that she had to leave for Europe. She had no clue what Europe was. She was excited but scared.

After a long journey Malika arrived and was welcomed by a woman in a uniform who knew two or three words from her native language: hello, please and thank you.

Malika was placed in a house with children of different ages and gender. Nora, the house owner, knew the basic words to communicate with her. She was from her original country but from another tribe. The children in the house were convinced that her tribe had caused the war. But she treated them all with respect and kindness. She was strict though, just like her mother. They did not dare to ask her about the war.

Malika was accepted into a local school. As she did not know the language she was put in a class with children who were far younger than her. She was the oldest and the tallest. She felt uncomfortable and was the subject of laughter in the class. Some children were horrible to her. Some of them told her that they didn't like her colour and clothes. She was unable to defend herself. This was the first time she was treated like that and she felt deeply disheartened.

Back at home before the war she always felt so special both in the school and at home. She was terrified of the idea that she had to live with this situation. She was worried because the teacher was not supportive either and was frustrated by her poor language and lack of confidence.

She struggled in the class with her studies, which made her more vulnerable and exposed. She was not sure whether she should tell Nora. She didn't have the confidence or the courage to talk about what was happening to her. She didn't know even how to describe what she was going through. She felt sick each single morning. She thought that happened because she couldn't sleep at night. She opted to keep silent but felt as if she was ripped open inside. She also hesitated to share this experience with her housemates. She just hated the school in silence until one day when she was approached by another girl in her class.

'I like you Malika. Would you like to come to my house?'

'Wouldn't your parents be angry if I came with you?' she asked in a low, hesitant voice.

'They know that I will invite you.'

Malika felt relieved. Her face lit up but she abruptly asked, 'Would they like my colour?'

'Don't be silly, of course they would. You are the kindest girl in the class. You are not mean and are willing to help anyone.' Since then they became best friends.

Malika spent quality time with Mandy's family but was unable to invite her back as she had no home of her own. She felt uneasy talking about it. 'We are not a real family. It was just a set of rules and punishments.' Malika convinced herself that this was a reasonable excuse not to invite Mandy back.

She always felt that the house was lacking a real soul. Some of the kids there were naughty and troublemakers. Nora was kind and caring but she had a lot on her plate and there was no dad in the house to support her like Mandy's family.

Mandy had never asked her about where she lived or who she lived with. She only took interest in whatever Malika was willing to discuss.

Malika felt happier when she joined Mandy's family on outings or a family game and always wished her parents were there. She was sad not knowing even if they were alive. She felt that one day she would find them, but dismissed the idea as a fancy dream.

Malika was unable to cope with the lessons and had to repeat the year, which meant that new kids would join her and the age gap between them would increase by a year. However, Mandy and her family helped Malika get through the year. They helped her with the homework and her command of the language. She improved steadily and managed to catch up with the rest of the class. She took additional lessons in her holidays.

Malika graduated from one of the best universities. On that day Malika opened her heart to Mandy and cried out her story.

Malika and Mandy applied together to join an international team that worked in her country. Both girls helped many of the vulnerable children but never looked at them as numbers or targets.

The country was still under the weight of the war more than twenty years after Malika had escaped the country. The villages were hardly rebuilt. The cities were in a poor state but the girls were determined to improve the quality of life for those who were less lucky.

Malika didn't give up her dream searching for her parents, but it remained a fanciful dream as she guessed. However, she was unable to bury the scene of her mother running behind the rising helicopter in the middle of a cloud of dust, which was generated by the departure of the helicopter.

The two friends set up an organisation that helped the victims of war. She turned her own story into a documentary to advocate against war of any kind. Their ideas were well supported and generated more funds. They managed to produce a series of true different stories. They followed the life journey of many victims, some of whom had fallen into the wrong hands and others had considerable achievements. The luckiest were those who managed to track down their families and compensate for the lost time. Sadly, Malika was not one of them.

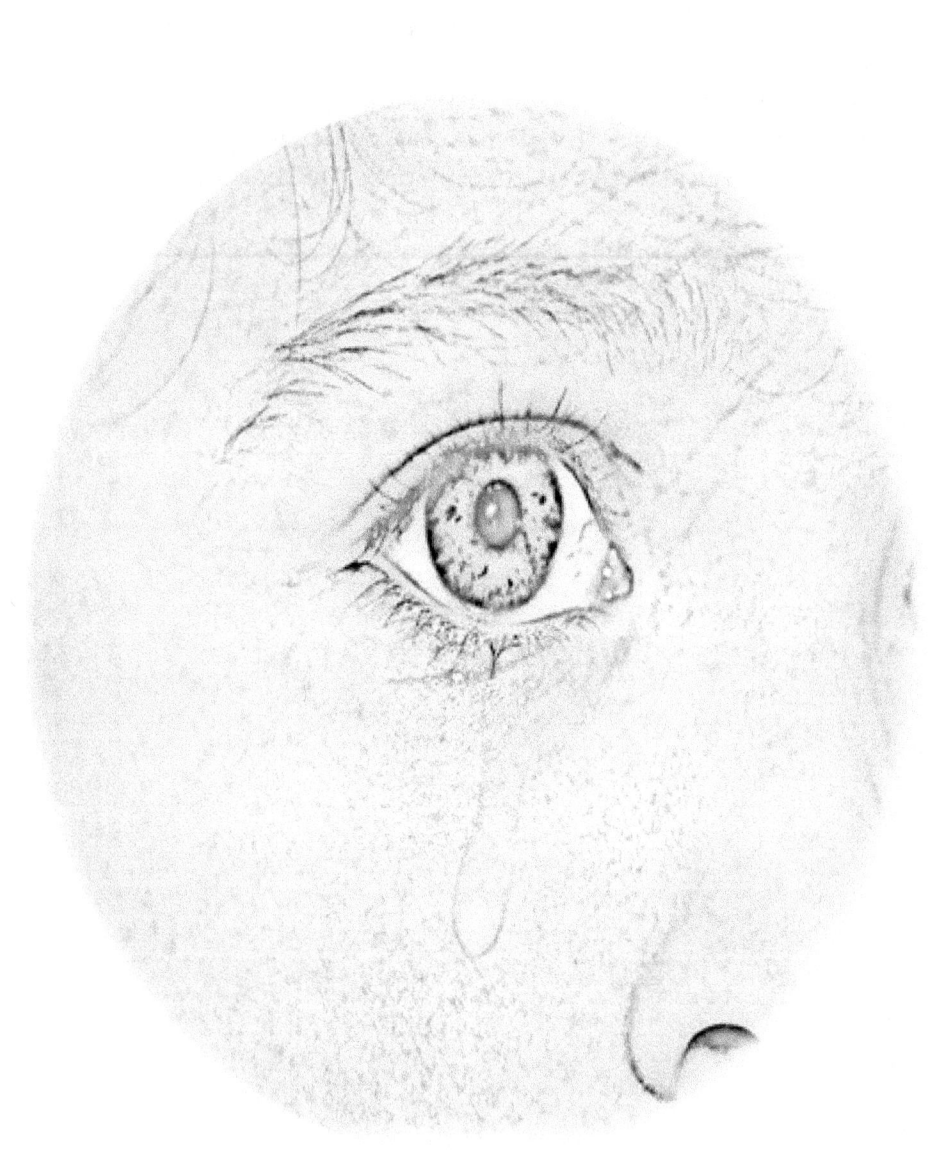

Our Mum is the Best,

No Matter What

Hassan and Hussein were twins who lived in one of the villages of the world. They grew up in a violent environment with an alcoholic and drug user father. Their mother Samira was a victim of domestic violence by her long-term drunk unemployed husband who sold her personal belongings, their furniture and forced her to beg her family for money.

Samira worked in a factory that manufactured shoes for export. Although the company which owned the factory made a lot of profit, the workers received very little for their hard work and long hours. They had no rights, incentives or protection. Their working environment was not safe. If they became ill they would be fired immediately.

At the end of every month Samira gave Raf, her husband, all her salary, otherwise she would get bruises and cuts, mostly in front of their children. Raf was always drunk. He blamed Samira and her family for his habits. He was forced to marry her after she was seen with him in a public place. He always thought that Samira was not the type of woman whom he would choose to be his wife. He didn't mind having a casual relationship with her but could not trust her as a wife. He always thought that she might have had relationships with other men, the way she had with him, though she didn't cross the line. She met with him for a coffee and a laugh and that was all.

Samira accepted her fate and was a loyal and tolerant wife. She had twins in their first year of marriage and had been a good mother to her twins. She took them to school, sorted out their problems and worked very hard to secure an income for the family.

One day Samira spent some of the money to buy an ice-cream for the boys. She noticed how their eyes followed the ice-cream cones in other children's hands, which caused her a great deal of grief. Hassan and Hussein were extremely happy to have this special treat. Samira was very pleased to see their faces lit with joy. With good intention she shared her pleasure with Raf, who felt provoked. He started shouting at her and throwing around whatever his hands grasped. Luckily enough the boys were not in the house. Samira was frightened. She begged him to stop but the situation escalated more and more. Her neighbour called the police and he was escorted away. Her family and Hassan blamed her for being beaten up. However, Hussein, the other twin, had always been close to his mother and seemed to understand the situation. He was relieved that his father was not there anymore.

Samira decided to take her twins and move to the city to start a new life. She was clear of one thing: relieve her family from what they perceived as a shame, as her story flew around in a fraction of a second like the spread of uncontrolled fire. She only told her sister, who helped her to leave the village under the cover of night. Her sister kept their arrangement secret from the family.

Samira and the twins had a very hard time at the beginning of their new life. She sold her marriage ring and her few jewels which were passed to her from her mother on her wedding day. This jewellery had belonged to her family for decades. No one knew how many years back since the custom of passing them down the line started. They only knew that each mother in the family passed them to her eldest daughter on her wedding night. It was deemed bad luck if they were lost. Knowing that, she was reluctant to lose them but she had no choice. She cried her soul out for many sleepless nights before her tears were literally dried out. She took her jewellery to the shop without looking back, to leave with a few pounds that didn't last for a week. However, the pain caused by the sense of guilt never settled. She lived with it for many years and she never told a soul about her ordeal.

Samira convinced herself that she would be forgiven for selling the family treasure as she was desperate for money to feed her boys. Anyway, she had no daughter to pass the jewellery onto. That was the first time she felt happy that she had no daughter, although she always hoped that she would have a daughter one day. She had chosen a name for her imaginary daughter, Jane. She dreamt about sewing Jane's colourful dresses and brushing her hair.

Samira contacted a charity that helped homeless families. They gave them a room and a meal each day. Samira sent her boys to a school near the charity premises. Hassan and Hussein were eligible for a free meal in the school. For her the only meal which she received from the charity kept her going till the next day. She lost a considerable amount of weight and always felt dizzy and tired.

Despite her poor health she spent long hours looking for jobs. She had no success as she had very limited skills. However, she remained positive and determined to learn new skills. She joined different classes which were run by the charity and volunteered to clean the rooms and wash the dishes after the lessons.

After a few months, Samira was allowed another meal as appreciation for her time and commitment. She always did more than what was expected of her.

The founder of the charity was impressed by her dedication. He offered her a paid job as a cleaner for their offices in addition to the rooms. She was lucky to be given that job. They also offered her another room for the boys.

At the end of the week when she received her first payment, she took the boys to the market and bought for them some second-hand clothes and trainers.

She also bought three cones of ice-cream to mark the end of a very distressing period in their life and to celebrate the new beginning.

The boys settled well in the school. Samira encouraged her children to do their homework regularly. She took an additional job in the nearby market. They felt happier but never talked about their father.

After a couple of months, Hassan started to act a bit strange. He neglected his homework and seemed withdrawn. She started to get letters from his teacher that he was not performing as expected of his age group. He was even disrupting the lessons and was behaving badly towards his teachers. Samira had no idea how to deal with him. She encouraged Hussein to talk to him but Hassan refused to interact with his brother. He had no friends and distanced himself from his mother. He shrugged his shoulders whenever his mother asked him about what was bothering him and never engaged in any conversations.

Samira was worried about her son. She wondered whether he was using drugs or was being bullied. She spoke with his teacher, took him to a doctor and even thought about returning to the village.

Hassan appeared fragile, angry and helpless. Witnessing the violence back at home and being unable to make sense of the situation left him feeling devastated. He lost connection with his own family as a result of the perceived brutal uprooting from his extended family.

He sincerely loved his mother because she had been there for them, whilst their father was engulfed in his bad habits but Hassan didn't want to talk about his feelings anymore. He couldn't see the point and believed that he was acting appropriately in his circumstances. He also distanced himself from his twin and any potential friend as if he wanted to run away from his past and present.

Hassan totally lost interest to interact with any human being as he blamed his mother for her choices; marrying his dad and taking them away from their family.

As Samira's worries grew she sought advice from a psychiatrist, who spoke to all of them individually before calling them to a family conference.

'We are here today because each of you found yourselves in an awkward situation and unable to understand why. You need to start opening up and take a joint decision if you are keen to save your family. I am sure you love each other dearly but you had to deal with a heavy burden, the impact of the addiction and the violence in the family. I understand that it was not an easy process, but you need to address these issues once and for all.' He then deliberately left the room.

Time stood still, with no sound to be heard apart from that arising from the friction between the forced out air and the nostrils.

Samira stuttered and failed to complete a sentence. She was convinced that this was the hardest moment in her entire life. She cleared her throat and took a deep breath.

She remembered the unlimited strength she developed when the midwife told her once to push harder as her twins were at risk of dying from lack of oxygen due to the lengthy delivery period. She certainly gave life to both of them when she made the strongest ever push.

Looking at Hassan she re-called the midwife's voice, 'Samira this is the last push for life.'

He was sitting on his chair with his arms crossed tightly over his chest but Samira could only see his tiny bluish head in the hands of the midwife. She closed her eyes, then very slowly opened them and pinched herself to make sure she was not dreaming.

'He needs that push now,' she whispered. 'I am really sorry I lost touch with you Hassan and left you struggling alone. I understand if you hate me.'

'Mum, I love you so much.' Hassan threw himself in her extended arms. 'I just missed the times when we had our family around; my aunties, uncles and cousins. I missed the outings and the fun. We were happier then.' He paused for a while before he suddenly said, 'I didn't bother about my dad. He doesn't belong to us. I never looked up to him. He made us suffer and never supported us. I am glad he is not with us. I am truly sorry that I failed to appreciate you. You have always been amazing and there for us.'

Samira was shocked. She always thought that Hassan was taking his father's side. She hugged him. He was like a lost angel who found himself trapped on earth.

Hussein sat quietly in his chair. Hassan looked at him for a moment. 'I am sorry bro. I lost my way all together. You dealt with everything just perfect. You get on well with Mum, that is why I felt you both let me down. Now I understand that was my way of dealing with my grief. I took it out on you. I shouldn't have. I compared myself to you and convinced myself that I am a loser. You managed to have friends, the teachers praised you and you were elected as the Head Boy.

'I was twisted at that time. I was unable to get rid of Dad. His shadow followed me everywhere. I felt so embarrassed by him as I was convinced that everybody else could see him. I hated the school, the teachers and my classmates.

'I was that close to turning into a younger copy of Dad. I was approached by young people who were older than me and had a lot of money, cigarettes and drugs. I met them outside the school when I skipped the lessons. They told me that they would replace my family and I would be respected if I join their gang.'

For the first time, and to Samira's astonishment, Hussein revealed his feelings, 'Mum I am sorry. I missed my dad but thought this will upset you so I never mentioned it. He followed me as well but I always kept your picture in my pocket.'

Hassan laughed and whispered, 'guess what, I did the same to get rid of him.' They laughed as they never had for a long time.

Samira wiped her tears and held the boys tight, 'you know what? We will get through this. We are a perfect family. We are stronger together. I couldn't have coped without you. I still need you. Each of you is a unique individual. Let us get out of here, we have a celebration to organise.

'I was paid extra money today. Would you like pizza, kebab or you prefer my cooking?' She laughed as they always joked that she was a terrible cook.

Two weeks after, Samira told her boys that she had good news for them. 'We are invited to visit our family. Your auntie is getting married. It would be a chance for you to see your dad and get to know him better. He is your dad anyway. If you don't want to go I understand.' She looked directly at them. A complete silence filled the room.

'Don't worry I will call my sister to tell her that we can't come.'

'No!' they shouted. 'We are just overwhelmed by the surprise. That's all.' The twins spoke at the same time. Samira was so happy that they were going back. She felt that she was a confident woman and the most proud Mum having two young lads looking up to her.

The night before the visit none of them was able to sleep. They had many issues to think about. The twins were not children anymore and Samira praised her ability to raise two children on her own. They were so resilient and sensible to the extent that they overcame the impact of the negative experience.

Both had joined a charity as volunteer mentors to support children and young people who were victims of domestic violence. They shared their experience and facilitated family conferences to empower them to resolve their issues in a friendly but well controlled environment. These conferences provided opportunities for violent parents to reflect on the impact of their actions on their families and themselves.

As a result of the twins' dedication and commitment many families were reformed or able to work out acceptable arrangements which were fair for all without being pushed to take extreme measures as Samira once did.

The twins remained convinced that family and friends were the key to a happier life, which comes in different shapes but free of violence and they chose 'Our Mum is the best' as their slogan and brand.

 # The Fall of the Mask

Nasma was her name, which means 'a gentle breeze'. The name accurately reflected her character. Like glass, she was gentle and fragile. Knowing her you would expect her to shatter into pieces facing the least cruel circumstances.

Feeling like an outsider within her family and close society, she dreamt of travelling the world searching for her identity beyond the geographical boundaries, language and religious beliefs. However, Nasma ended up confined to a small corner of a local library in Port-Sudan, the city that enjoys the cuddle of the Red Sea.

A librarian was the only employment opportunity she could get. Her family welcomed the fact that she became a breadwinner to support the many open mouths which needed feeding. Nasma grew up in a large family, which was difficult for the father, the only working member, to maintain.

Although Nasma's father encouraged his children to take their education seriously, higher education remained an unreachable dream for most of her generation. The opportunities were limited by the fierce competition for the scarce resources.

Many talented students were unable to pursue their dreams because of the high cost of living away from their families with no support systems. The universities were concentrated in the capital and the largest cities.

Nasma spent her free time day-dreaming, wandering the streets of the world, enjoying her relationship with Mother Nature and communicating with God in her own way.

On a particular day, Nasma felt attracted to a customer who chose a quiet corner in her library to examine a number of rare books which she kept on a special shelf. Salah, the customer, had taught himself to become a deep sea diver.

Over a period of time, Nasma and Salah developed a unique relationship and became soul mates. They spent their break time discussing shared ideas. He spoke little about himself apart from the fact that he left his family at a young age looking for pleasure and had never returned.

At times Nasma felt that Salah was selfish and lacked beliefs and values in the way she had. But something there connected them. Deep down she knew what that thing was, but never talked about, maybe due to lack of confidence or courage. Maybe she felt she could challenge and influence his behaviour.

Salah brought back Nasma's childhood memories, though she hardly remembered anything apart from a journey on a boat with a transparent floor with her family. It was like a fairytale. She was not certain though whether the journey was a real part of her memory or a dream. Never mind, the sea-bed was so colourful and beautiful, full of different breath-taking species, rocks and plants. She wanted so badly to dive into the deep-end. She saw herself transformed into a mermaid swimming alongside Salah. For a second she wondered if that was a dream, future prediction or destiny?

His voice was real and warm, 'Yes, I know you. We were so close. We had something special but just before we devoted ourselves to each other, I lost you forever.'

She was trembling from head to toe and felt as warm as his voice. She realised that she could still read his mind but for some reason he was so distant and indecisive like the old days.

Suddenly, a cold and lifeless voice brought her back to reality, 'What do you say?' Sami, her future husband, whispered. He was part of an arranged marriage by both families.

Nasma replied with a hollow voice and emptiness inside. 'Yes ... let us give it a try.'

She spent a lot of time, day and night, thinking and sinking, whether it was her last chance to find or lose her identity forever.

She talked a lot about her unique and extreme ideas as if she wanted to push him away. Sami accepted all her conditions and unrealistic requests with enthusiasm and ease. Nasma felt insecure but hoped that luck was within her grasp.

Sami pushed hard for their big day, together with her family. The day arrived sooner than she expected. It was not what she hoped for but was special. For the first time ever Nasma felt happy without any worries masking her happiness. She felt that this time was different, though there were many factors that could have brought negative thoughts to the surface. It seemed as if these factors were locked away.

Nasma and her husband started a promising life together full of excitement and success. But have they coped?

Nasma wrote to her friend, Salma, 'Guess what. I am full of joy. I did not need to change. I am myself and as happy as a baby', but she never sent the message because the mask had fallen apart very fast.

The agreed conditions were torn apart and evaporated. The past haunted the present. Life became agonizing. The dreams were shattered like broken glass. The varied expectations grabbed both of them by the throat.

Nasma struggled to keep up and come to terms with her new life. She had to pretend to be happy, to avoid the anger storms, whilst her soul died every day. This meant that the muscles of her face were forcibly contracted to forge a smile or laughter. She suffered mental distress trying to engage with meaningless discussions and absorb the huge culture gap. She wondered how to break the vicious cycle and spent long sleepless and lonely nights in deep fear not only from her husband but from herself too. She felt like a prisoner in their bed. Horrific ideas crossed her mind but she was unable to face the consequences. She had lost control of her life.

Nasma felt outraged when she discovered that her husband blamed her for their failure to have children, knowing that he was infertile. 'That was the straw that broke the camel's back'. She became lifeless and confused. The small remaining portion of her happiness slowly disappeared. Her ability to react diminished and her movement became sluggish. Grey hair crawled over her head. Dark circles decorated her eyes. But it was not clear whether she had totally lost hope.

Nasma intensively prayed to God to save her, but it seemed as if her prayers lost their way. However, despite the gloomy picture, a glimpse of hope and a flow of faith grew inside her.

Once she decided to disobey her husband's rule, not to leave the house without his permission. She desperately needed to defuse the mounting anger which lately filled her entire body and drove her into anger fits.

Passing in front of her library Nasma felt an unusual wave of warmth that gave her an unlimited strength. She heard an inner voice encouraging her to go inside. It wasn't an easy decision or her favourite moment either passing through the automatic door. She didn't feel the same. She was clumsy, hesitant but at ease.

High she lifted her right foot and leant forward like a baby who is desperate to learn how to walk and prematurely tried to take their first step. Nasma was about to fall but she managed to hold on to the access ramp and proudly smiled.

The faces appeared different, their features were not so clear but their welcoming, 'How can I help you?' was like a romantic melody to her ears.

She smiled easily as the books filled with joy at her return. The special shelf with the rare books cried with happiness. And for the first time in many years a tiny tear ran across her cheek declaring the return of the real Nasma. It was a true stream of feelings that had been kept static for a long time. Without thinking Nasma looked at the quiet, but empty corner, where Salah, the deep-sea diver, used to sit exploring the rare books from her special shelf.

Moments passed slowly before Nasma realised that another mask had fallen apart but not so fast this time. Her chest expanded to allow fresh air to replace the rotten soggy air which had been trapped inside her for a decade.

Nasma's prayers were finally responded to in a predestined time.

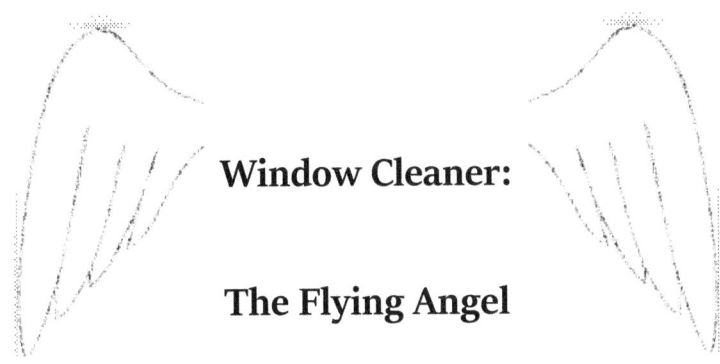

Window Cleaner:

The Flying Angel

'Caution — cleaning overhead'. Tom ran past the square sign to catch the overcrowded lift. He was gasping for air. The train journey had been one from hell. He had an appointment at 9 a.m. with an inspector and it was half past nine already.

He couldn't call the office earlier because the train was stuck in the tunnel and his phone battery was flat anyway.

Yesterday, he had gone to bed very late after reading the report which he prepared for the meeting. This morning he woke up with a headache and was lacking concentration.

He was in a great hurry but had missed his bus because he forgot his glasses and had to return home to collect them. Tom had to wait another fifteen minutes for the next bus. As a result he was late for his train.

'Mind the gap, the train is ready to depart', but it never did! It was the hottest day since records began. The carriage was fully packed with angry commuters who breathed directly into each other's noses and competed for the small amount of fresh air.

Tom was annoyed by the endless mobile conversations around him. 'Sorry darling, I can't make it. The train is running late and moving extremely slow. There was a faulty train ahead of us. You take the kids and I will join you later.'

'Dad, the train is late, there was a signal failure. We've waited for fifty minutes on the platform. It has just arrived'.

'Sorry mate. We were stuck in the tunnel and the driver gave up. He stopped updating us and we were left in the dark.'

Tom tuned out all the chat and buried his head in a newspaper. He read all the gossip in town.

He pushed the slowly moving automatic door in a futile attempt to race time. The door stopped for a short time, before it started again. The push interrupted the system and it had to re-adjust and then continued progressing in a stiff way. However, it seemed to Tom as if it had stopped forever.

Tom jumped the waiting queue for the lift. His colleagues were not happy with his action. He tried to explain why he jumped the queue but his explanations were irrelevant.

'Sorry I am late.'

In reflection he silently retrieved and scanned all the excuses he presented to his manager for being late: 'I have already received a warning; it is the responsibility of all employees to make their own arrangements to come to work on time, though the train is my only means of transport.

'I used all the possible excuses but a late train was not one of them. It was never counted as a credible reason for arriving late to work. Managers see that as beyond the planning process.'

The inspector had gone. 'I guess it is grounds for a disciplinary!'

'Poor me,' he thought as he took a sip from his hot and very strong black coffee to mask the events of the morning. He made a slurping sound, which annoyed his nearby colleagues in the open-space office.

Tom lifted his heavy eyes and looked towards the window.

He saw his flying angel, the window cleaner in his white overall and wings moving up and down his glass window, which was so clean and shiny.

This scene brought back a memory of his childhood when he was six years old. He recalled his conversation with his mother.

'Mammy, I saw the flying angel today. I spoke to him through a gap in the curtains. He is not a stranger, right?

'He always listens to me, though he can't see me. He was in a bright white overall. I think he has wings. Not sure though. He moves up and down our window with his magic stick. I guess he was cold and needed a warm bed like mine.

'I think he wanted to find out why I was sad and on my own.

'I was sad because there was a group of scary boys who took the fairy cakes that you baked especially for me and my favourite sandwiches from my lunch box. They left me only the fruits and yoghurt.

'They told me that my lunch was so yummy that they wanted to share it with me. They told me not to tell any teacher or parent because they would be angry with me.

'I promised them I wouldn't.

'I thought these boys were my friends because they scared the other children. They also told me that their parents can't afford to buy a packed lunch for them. I felt really bad. They do not look different to me.

'I can't understand why their parents cannot afford to give them packed lunches. They can't explain that either.

'Mum, I only told the flying angel that I always had a tummy ache. He kind of listened to me and was not angry because I shared my lunch with my friends.

'I needed to talk to someone.

'They can't hurt an angel, right Mum?

'He is strong and kind and has magical powers.'

'Tom,' a harsh angry voice penetrated his ears. 'You have not sent the report yet. What are you thinking? It is already late. We need to talk.'

Tom pressed the mouse so hard that his computer froze. He gazed at the window and waved goodbye to his angel as he flew up towards the next floor.

Remembering the old days when he stood behind the curtains waiting for his flying angel inspired him to do something to help others desperately waiting behind their curtains for someone to share their anxieties with.

He decided to support a local anti-bullying group. He chose window cleaning as his challenge to raise funds for the group. He joined a window cleaning team at the tallest building in the city, though he was afraid of heights.

On the fundraising day he put on his white overall, locked the harness and set off. He was scared but happy to be identified by many kids as their flying angel. He was once impressed by a window cleaner, who was there for him when he was reluctant to talk to his mother or a teacher about the scary boys.

Tom was very pleased to be able to raise one thousand pounds for his charity.

Later he was chosen by the charity as an ambassador to raise awareness of the impact of bullying on school children. He shared his story with the children but encouraged them to talk about bullying to their teachers or parents besides the flying angel, the window cleaner.

The Stillbirth

Marriage

Ayda was born prematurely and never caught up with the mental level of her siblings, though it was not that obvious to an outsider. She lived with a heavy burden of abuse from her own family. She was teased about her lack of concentration and short memory especially by her older sister. She tried to compensate for that by caring about what other people expected of her and neglecting her inner needs. She suffered in silence and very much hated herself and no doubt appeared to people as being indifferent.

When she set free her imagination she was perceived as lying and a classmate competitor never shied away from labelling her in front of anybody in attendance. This attitude frustrated her most as the bully classmate enjoyed putting down everyone around her. She was full of herself as the genius of all times, never to mention her lack of sensitivity, decency and human touch. When younger Ayda suffered fits when her body was burning with fever, her sister dismissed them as fake attempts to grab her mother's attention. Luckily enough she was totally recovered without damaging consequences and led a normal life apart from two unrelated to her fits of psychological distortions that affected her entire life. One was the impact of the circumcision, the surgical removal of parts of the genital system of young girls in accordance with a strong cultural belief. The other was the unreasonable punishment she received when she started to discover her senses and body and apparently allowed a local boy to hold her hands in public.

Then Ayda was pushed into a marriage with a wealthy business-man, who was lacking the basic level of moral conscience but was able to lift her family above the poverty line.

She was a good looking young lady with deep brown eyes and long, dark rich hair. Additionally, she was a first class chef and a great host, who most men would fall for.

All that she needed was some time to adapt to the new life and get over her psychological hurdles but that was not what her husband believed he had paid for. He took her behaviour badly and tried to break the silence by all means.

Ayda felt horrified by the lack of understanding which pushed her further away. She experienced a huge amount of physical and psychological pain. A lot of accusations were thrown in her face. She was extremely unhappy and felt as if she was morally raped and that their marriage was shattered and the trust was faded.

For three lengthy years they pretended they were the happiest couple. They were seen as a role model for a very successful mar-riage. He bought her jewellery, shoes and dresses and took her on luxury trips but the physical pain remained the constant feature of their nights as the barrier never shied away in the absence of the passion and the lack of receptiveness.

The advisors from both families on how to make babies stuck their noses into their personal life.

'Ayda I know a brilliant doctor who could help you have a baby,' said her cousin.

'Don't worry Safa, it is not meant to happen yet.'

Many family members volunteered to accompany them to differ-ent specialists in the fertility clinics of the city. But they alone knew the bare truth.

One afternoon her mother-in-law took the liberty to invite a doctor she knew to have a dinner with her in their house.

'Ayda, our family is known for its fertility. It is our honour on the line. You have been married now for three years, and no sign of babies. Our patience is running out.'

Ayda was so hurt but out of respect she agreed to talk to the doctor. When she was alone with her husband she confronted him, 'did you know about your mother's plans to invite this doctor?'

'Of course, I agree with her. My patience is running out as well.'

'I feel I was let down by your behaviour. Are you seeing somebody else?'

'Well then let us see a marriage councillor.'

'Are you joking?' Omer walked up and down the room with his hands in his pockets. With a shaky high tone voice he said, 'what nonsense you are suggesting?' He looked at her and continued, 'What am I going to say to him? What a shame? Have you thought about my feelings? Have you thought about my pride? We are subject to laughter and gossip in every home: the neighbours, the friends, my job mates and even your family.

'Mother is right you know, there is a long queue of girls who are younger and more beautiful than you waiting out there for any man to marry them.'

Ayda didn't hide her frustration and felt sick.

'You will end up a lonely, old and ugly woman. Then you will pay for your stupidity and arrogance.' He left the house and didn't come back that night.

That was the night when for the first time the memories, when she was only a few years old, came back to haunt her. She felt that pain when she had to go through the unjustified practice of performing her circumcision. She couldn't understand why everybody was happy, elegantly dressed, covered with nice perfumes when she was bleeding and experiencing a huge physical pain. The family members, neighbours and friends were kissing her and placing money under her pillow just like the tooth fairy which seems happy that a child lost a tooth. She herself was dressed in a colourful, silky night dress and put on a specially decorated bed. Everyone cheered when the special lady declared that she was circumcised.

A woman singer with a drum was singing all day with women and girls dancing around her in a designated area and giving her a lot of money when the singer sang her name and the name of her close family.

A man slaughtered a lamb, which is the only one that felt her pain as it experienced a far greater pain than hers. Its pain cost it its life but provided happiness in the day. Her pain also provided happiness for all around her on that day but caused misery around her many years after.

The older women gathered under a bunker, which had been erected in the yard to protect them from the day's heat. They were busy cooking nice food. The younger girls prepared lots of coffee and tea for the working women and took around trays of sweets, dates and home-made juice.

From the smell, Ayda could tell that the food was of a high quality but she had no appetite and ate nothing for two days. She cried all day. It was a horrible experience but she appreciated the money she was given.

She was left in the shadow three years after their wedding when he decided to have another wife. He went along the aisle with a total stranger who was interested only in his money. He got drunk to silence his loss, frustration and disappointment. However, he pretended that he didn't mind the false victory as he long ago lost his confidence.

Ayda preferred not to fight her corner at that time. She had apparently given up. Omer seemed happier but didn't treat his new wife with dignity. He lived with a hope that he might reach reconciliation with Ayda. However, she was forced to leave her bedroom and move to a distant part of the house. She found a job and her relationship with her husband was put on hold. He didn't offer to divorce her and she didn't bother to ask for it.

Lost and Found

The Lapse of Faith

Sama was born into a very religious but liberal family. She struggled to balance the controversy between society's interpretation of faith and that which she inherited. She was surprised that within her religion people from different parts of the world held diverse views about the same God. Sama wished that the religious interpretation of concepts was as clear-cut as one plus one equals two with no shadow of doubt.

This conflict shaped her life and the way her faith was once lost but miraculously found. She always felt that she was cramped in a tight piece of space on the edge of the endless universe.

Sama held a view that in schools officials built barriers around religious studies and wondered why? She concluded that the content might have been overwhelmingly holy that people were unable to handle.

Sama defined children as curious by nature but felt that no concrete answers were offered to satisfy their curiosity about God. For her that was human nature dealing with the unknown. She saw God's power as immense, whilst human capacity is so limited. Like every other child in her class, Sama learnt by heart what she was taught, but was not necessarily able to make sense of it.

She spent countless nights listening to her grandfather magnificently humming religious verses, which he strongly believed were the words of God. She never understood the meaning of the words but enjoyed every moment listening to these verses. She experienced pleasant feelings but was unable to understand what was happening to her. Even when she was grown up she was too frightened to express her feeling in a world that saw faith and religion as obstacles and threats.

In her mind religious people like her were judged by many as having limited brain capacity, living in an imaginary world and lacking scientific evidence when it came to faith. She wondered whether science and technology were able to explain the entire life systems beyond the big bang moment.

Sama believed that there was a fine line between those who have an ultra-vision and those who limit themselves to material evidence only. However, she was convinced that spirituality and faith were the winners in this comparison.

Growing up in a society that was fast changing towards high material consumption and quick profit, Sama felt an ideological dilemma had crawled in to her life as the value of the human being was measured by the level of his or her income and their technological capability. She was terrified by the concept of left or right, good or bad as the moral compass and black or white as the colour of life with no shade of grey.

'Peace be upon you,' Sama greeted strangers, the way she used to do back home, but none cared. During her life journey, Sama came into contact with people who suffered through no fault of their own due to wars, famine and natural disasters. She witnessed people being hurt because they were created black, with ginger hair or disabled. She was disheartened by people who undermined fellow citizens for a political gain or just ignorance.

Although Sama felt that the earth was eager to welcome the tears of the sky to wash out the misery of planet earth she recognised the deep crack that pushed its way through the banks of the longest river and smacked the children on the face. She witnessed the children picking up their distended bellies and sliding peacefully into a coma alleviating their malnourished bodies and souls from a long-standing agony. She saw a small boy being stabbed to death with no apparent motive apart from racism but the case collapsed before it reached the court. Sama didn't comprehend why some people were born slaves but others billionaires.

These thoughts disturbed her to the extent that she questioned the purpose of life. That was the breaking point when Sama realised that her faith had gone forever and she felt totally empty. She dropped her arms carelessly and let it go.

With no hesitation, Sama assumed that she had limited brain capacity and was living in an imaginary hollow bubble that lacked scientific evidence as perceived by some influential people. And since then she took things as they came.

Sama didn't feel comfortable or calm. On the contrary she was irritated and felt frightened. Inside her, mixed emotions were cultivated and built up to a volatile level. Her head expanded and was about to explode when finally she decided to look for the lost faith. After searching everywhere and examining every corner in the world she gave up and lost hope. She felt sad and miserable.

During her journey in search for her lost faith, Sama worked on a cruise ship. For many long misty nights she felt as if the sea was her bed and the sky was her blanket with nobody else around. That gave her an opportunity to search deep into her soul for the lost faith.

Whenever the vessel reached land, Sama interacted with different creations of God. She spent long hours examining the soil, trees, pandas and buds. She stared at spiders' webs and honeycombs. She followed an elegant trail of ants patiently carrying loads of winter's supplies twice their weight.

She was charmed by the harmony between the warm earth and the fluffy white snow. She chased a cheerful insect dancing around a bunch of flowers to a tune of a canary.

Sama enjoyed the laughter of innocent babies but not the screams of women, struggling to push life into the world having carried it for nine months of joy and pain.

One night Sama felt brain-bloated and decided to go early to her cabin. She whispered a few verses which she had learnt from her grandfather to protect her from evil. She smiled and turned onto her right side and went into a deep sleep.

Sama suddenly woke up. It was completely dark and silent. She couldn't see her fingers but was able to smell the ground above her. She assumed that she had died and was in her grave.

'Am I waiting for judgement day?' she whispered. 'But why haven't the angels questioned me when I was laid into my grave as our teacher taught us?'

She looked up as if she was talking directly to God. 'You assured us that we will be judged by our intentions. My intentions have always been genuine. I wanted to understand your mighty power. I believed that I could help people realise your existence in ways that they can relate to and accept. I tried to find scientific evidence to assure myself that I am not obsolete.' Sama continued her dialogue with God. 'I can't understand why our traditions and ways of life were always dismissed as having no value whatsoever.

'I am concerned that the cultures in some part of the world were undermined until they were re-discovered by the influential nations then the same practices became highly appreciated, fashionable, glorified and accepted as the norm.'

Sama was convinced that hundreds of years ago her religion believed in breastfeeding and promoted it amongst the orphans encouraging women to volunteer their milk. However, she also realised the benefit of the industrial revolution, which needed more working hands as the world wars claimed more men than women. She was furious that the men with the greatest power turned to the breastfeeding women who threw their breasts away and joined in as they were told that breastfeeding damages the 'size zero' figure, which was every woman's dream.

Sama smiled and took pride in the fact that her great-grandparents, their children and grandchildren were breastfed. In her forties, she can still remember the taste of her mother's milk which as a child she found rich and delicious. She thought highly of her healthy upbringing, which was disregarded once by influential people. She certainly wondered why the importance of breastfeeding had suddenly been reinstated and turned into an obsession. It was all over the place; the main health establishment, among researchers and institutions, the Internet and social media, the mass media of the era.

A gentle hand touched Sama taking her away from her thoughts and guided her through a narrow passage beneath their family home.

For a moment she thought it was the hand of God. But as she heard an echo of the verses which she used to love as a child, Sama immediately recognised her grandfather's voice.

She experienced the same pleasant feeling listening to these verses. She couldn't see him but felt the presence of his spirit safeguarding her.

She wondered whether her grandfather had been watching over her and witnessed her faith being stolen. Sama strongly believed that her granddad's spirit had driven her towards finding her faith. She was also convinced that his soul had foreseen her thoughts and doubts.

Sama opened her eyes slowly and felt each movement of her eye-lids. She saw an intangible figure of her grandfather. She struggled to reach his hand as it rose higher and higher.

She forcefully lifted her body and extended her back as far as her muscles permitted. She stood on the tips of her toes as if she was ready to take-off, but the figure continued to elevate. It seemed to her so remote that she could only see a glittering bundle of light that pushed back the darkness.

Her arms were fully extended upwards with the fingers curved inwards trying to catch the bright speedy light. Her body was covered with sweat. Her breathing was fast and shallow. Her heart was about to jump out and her muscles were as stiff as solid rocks.

She looked miserable but welcomed the return of her lost faith, the glittering bundle of light. She felt relieved as if the weight of the whole world had been lifted from her shoulders.

Sama jumped from her bed as the captain announced the end of their journey. The ship reached the port of her country. She wept loudly and laughed at the same time as she saw as many happy faces than she had ever seen before.

If You Wonder Who I Am

I am a product of mixed civilizations, cultures and identities. I am Africa, Europe, Asia, America and much more. My family was nick-named the mini-united nations; a vast collection of nationalities, religions, languages, visions, experiences … a colour spectrum from every corner of the globe.

What unites us is our humanity, principles, selflessness, courage, honesty and passions.

Search deep into your soul and you will find something in common with me; in your dreams, consciousness, moments of happiness and sadness or just when feeling flat.

I was deeply affected by peoples' sufferings and hurts facing injustice, discrimination, abuse, prejudice and exclusion. I am also humbled by their resilience.

I would like to share some thoughts about me from those who crossed my path in different capacities.

'I have found her to be a sober, polite, well-mannered and a strong charactered individual.'

'I found her very technically sound, hard working and extremely professional.'

'She is very sociable and very excellent in establishing and maintaining interpersonal relationships.'
'She is a very warm-hearted and good-natured lady. She is kind, reflective and responsible in her words and actions and has always been polite.'

'She is a friendly, thoroughly reliable, honest and enthusiastic individual.'

*'I have always been impressed with her courage
to not just confront prejudices facing her
but also in her support to others.'*

Thank you for believing in me. All the above couldn't have happened if not for my late mother and father and my extended family.

My message to my readers:
I hope you have enjoyed the glance into my soul without passing judgement ... I am just a human being.

Being optimistic, I hope that each one of you found just a line, a hint, a word or a thought that relates to you or inspires you to make a change, no matter how small it is.

Even if you just shed a tear, had a smile, felt connected to me or just had a drop of sweat on your forehead, reading my words, thank you.